THEODORE REX

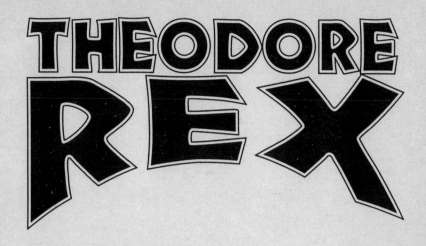

A novelization by J.J. Gardner
Based on the motion picture written by Jonathan Betuel

SCHOLASTIC INC.
New York Toronto London Auckland Sydney

ISBN 0-590-67786-1

Photo Credits
All interior photos Suzanne Hanover
Cover photo of Theodore Rex by Blake Little
Cover photo of Whoopi Goldberg by Suzanne Hanover

12 11 10 9 8 7 6 5 4 3 2 1   5 6 7 8 9/9 0/0

Printed in the U.S.A.   40

First Scholastic printing, December 1995

THEODORE REX

"A dino's in trouble!" cried Theodore "Teddy" Rex as he woke from the nightmare in alarm. The dream had startled him so much that even the scales on his ten-foot-long tail were shaking.

Teddy knew instantly that his nightmare was no ordinary dream. Ever since dinosaurs had been genetically cloned and laboratory-hatched, they had come into this world with a special ability, a sixth sense if you will, that tingled whenever one of their kind was in danger.

And now Teddy's sixth sense was tingling like crazy.

Disturbed, he reached over to the night table next to his bed and dialed the holophone. A human police operator's face appeared in full 3-D in the tiny window on the phone.

"Grid Police Headquarters," said the police operator. "Voice ID please?"

"This is Teddy Rex," the dinosaur replied anxiously. "I just had a *flash*. It was like I was being chased through the dark. It woke me up from a dead sleep."

"Sounds like you had too many cookies before bed," said the police operator with a smirk. "Turn over."

Teddy sighed. "I don't think so," he insisted impatiently. "Check the duty reports. See if anything's happened."

That was just like a human, not to believe in *dino-flashes*, Teddy thought as he waited anxiously for the police operator to check the computer.

"Let's see here," said the police operator. "Just the usual mayhem. Wait a minute. Here's something. We have a report of an explosion in the Carnival Graveyard near Prehistoric Place. Apparently there's a dino involved."

Teddy snapped the three stubby toes on one of his feet as his suspicions were confirmed. "I'm on my way," he told the police operator. Then he hung up the holophone and leaped out of bed.

CLANG! He smashed his head into the low-hanging ceiling pipe just as he did every time he got out of bed. Sometimes Teddy forgot that he was an eight-foot-tall, three-thousand-pound Tyrannosaurus with a heavy tail, and that most apartments were made for humans who were usually a lot smaller than he was.

Teddy opened the refrigerator in search of a quick energy snack. Fortunately he had just made a fresh bowl of his favorite cookie dough the night before so he stuffed a few globs into his automatic cookie toaster and set the timer. Then he slipped on a clean turtleneck sweater, his favorite jeans (the ones with the knee patches sewed on) and his brand-new, *triple-E*-width pro-Keds, size 176. By the time he had finished dressing, the cookies were ready. One by one they shot out of the toaster and into his eagerly waiting mouth. He put the last few aside for later.

Teddy would have made a second batch of cookies, but there was no time. He grabbed his coat and shades and said a quick good-bye to his dog, Zippy. Then he winked at the poster of his favorite fictional dino, detective Sam O. Saurus (he had read every Sam O. Saurus mystery novel ever printed), and punched a code into the security terminal on the front door.

The Rex Cruiser barreled through the streets of the Grid at a fantastic speed with Teddy at the wheel. Teddy's car was a souped-up police car designed for visitors' tours. It had a special compartment for its driver's tail, both rear and front wheel drive, and a special twenty-four-cylinder engine that was designed to carry the weight of the hulking dino.

In a few moments Teddy reached the Carnival Graveyard and brought the cruiser to a screeching halt. Police cars were gathered around and Teddy could see that several detectives were already at work inside a barricaded section of the street.

Something awful had happened, Teddy realized. He felt the scales on his tail shiver.

A human onlooker was trying to get a peek

through the barricade as Teddy got out of the car and approached the scene.

"A dead dino?" he heard the onlooker ask a rookie police officer who was standing guard.

"Move out," the rookie told the onlooker. "Show's over."

"Why would someone kill a dino?" the onlooker asked in a sad tone of voice. "They don't hurt anyone."

"If you like 'em so much," the rookie cop replied with a snide laugh, "why don't you go down to Prehistoric Place where the rest of the *scales* live?"

"That's not a nice thing to say, officer," Teddy said as he came up behind the rookie.

The rookie turned around. "What's it to you, *scale*?" asked the cop.

Teddy pulled out his Grid Police Department badge and held it up. "Rex, Teddy Rex," Teddy announced, "Grid P.D. Public Relations. We're not *scales*. We're *dinos*. How would you like it if I called you *softskins*?"

Teddy normally tried to treat everyone with respect. As a public relations officer it was his job to give a good impression of dinos to a sometimes prejudiced public. But his job became even tougher when he came across police officers who didn't like dinos. And, as Teddy had come to learn since he joined the force, there were many.

He supposed it wasn't easy for humans. After

all, up until a generation ago they had the run of the planet. They had thought of dinosaurs as long since extinct, the species of some long-ago epoch. But ever since the regeneration of many dinosaur species and their evolution into intelligent beings, dinosaurs lived side by side with humans.

Teddy shouldered past the rookie cop and entered the cordoned-off area of the crime scene. Flashbulbs were going off as the police photographer took pictures. As Teddy got closer he saw what they were taking pictures of. It was the huge body of a dinosaur, the one Teddy had seen in his *flash*. Now it was lying flat on its back, dead.

"He a Grid-mate of yours, Teddy?" He heard someone ask him.

Teddy glanced up. It was Sarah Jiminez, a detective he knew from headquarters.

"Yes and no," replied Teddy.

"You lost me," said the detective.

"Well," began Teddy, "I was asleep when all of a sudden I had a flash something was wrong."

"Oh, right," nodded Detective Jiminez with understanding. "The *dino-sense* . . ."

"We call it *empathy*," explained Teddy. "All dinos are on the same wavelength."

"Till someone took *him* off the air," said the detective, pointing to the dead dino.

"A dinocide," muttered Teddy. "That's never happened before. Extinction, yes, but — "

"Hey, this is the Grid," shrugged Detective

Jiminez. "We have universal health care, guaranteed housing, *and* free cable. But crime still happens."

Teddy couldn't stop staring at the victim. "Do you have any clues?" he asked.

"No suspects, evidence, or leads," replied the detective. "Our first John Doe dino."

Teddy pulled out his portable holophone and switched it on. "Headquarters," he said, speaking into it, "where is Commissioner Lynch?"

"He's off duty tonight," replied the police operator.

"It's an emergency," insisted Teddy. "I need to find him."

After a moment the police operator said: "He's at a New Eden fund-raiser at the Explorers Club."

"I'm on my way," said Teddy. Then he switched off his phone, climbed back into the Rex Cruiser, and sped off toward one of the wealthiest sections of the Grid. A section where dinosaurs were very seldom welcome.

"Teddy Rex," Teddy announced himself to the butler as he entered the Explorers Club lobby. From where he stood Teddy could see that a posh party was in full swing in the ballroom. It was clearly for humans only — and *rich* ones at that.

"I'm sorry," replied the butler snobbishly. "This is an invitation-only affair."

Teddy didn't have time for explanations. He flashed his badge and pushed past the butler. No sooner had he approached the ballroom than he was stopped by Deputy Commissioner Alex Summers, a small man who smelled as if he had taken a bath in a vat of very bad cologne. The man acted as if he were happy to see Teddy, but Teddy knew otherwise.

"Teddy. What a surprise," Summers said with a false note in his voice. "Here to work the room?"

"Hello, Deputy Commissioner," said Teddy. "Sorry to barge in." Teddy extended his tail and shook Summers's hand.

"I didn't know you were a million-credit-chip donor to the New Eden Ecology Foundation," said Summers.

"I'm not," replied Teddy, hiding his astonishment at the high price of admission. "On my take-home I can barely pay my rent. I'm looking for Commissioner Lynch. Ah, there he is now. Nice talking to you, Mr. Summers."

Teddy eased away from the deputy commissioner and waddled his way into the main ballroom. Teddy could feel all the eyes in the room fall on him as he entered. A dino at an expensive fund-raiser like this was clearly an unexpected sight.

Teddy didn't let the human stares bother him. Maybe he didn't have a million credit chips to offer the Ecology Foundation, but that wasn't going to stop him from reaching his goal. Someone had killed a dino for the first time in the Grid's history. He had to see Commissioner Lynch and he had to see him *now*.

Commissioner Lynch, looking distinguished in his tuxedo, rose from his table as Teddy approached.

"Teddy?" he asked, surprised to see the T-Rex.

"Commissioner Lynch," said Teddy. "There's been a murder in the Carnival Graveyard, sir."

Before Commissioner Lynch could respond, they were approached by an elderly man, a man Teddy knew to be Elizar Kane.

"Elizar Kane," began Commissioner Lynch. "May I present Teddy Rex, Assistant Press Liaison Officer with the Grid Police Department."

Mr. Kane smiled at Teddy. "Teddy and I go back a ways," he said warmly.

Teddy smiled, too. "Not many of us get to meet our maker."

Teddy watched as the realization hit Lynch. "Of course!" he exclaimed. "You recreated dinosaurs, didn't you, Mr. Kane?"

"Yes, I did," admitted Kane. "And of them all, Teddy is my crowning achievement. He must be an asset to your department."

"Gee, I try, Mr. Kane," Teddy said, his scales turning red with humility.

Just then Dr. Shade, an attractive woman Teddy knew to be Mr. Kane's personal physician, stood up at her table. "And now," she announced to everyone, "it is my honor to present Elizar Kane: DNA research pioneer and founder of the New Eden ecology movement."

As Kane made his way to the head of the table, Teddy noticed that the room fell into a respectful silence.

"Years ago," Kane began when he was sure all eyes were on him, "I recreated dinosaurs to show how science could change the world. My New

Eden Foundation developed disease-resistant crops. We helped to outlaw private cars and fossil fuels."

At that everyone applauded, including Teddy. Kane's accomplishments were indeed impressive.

Kane continued: "But as you know, over time, our cities outgrew their names. Our world became an endless grid of streets. My dream is a return to paradise. My friends, I believe it is possible — thanks to your generous contributions, of course!"

Once again everyone applauded. Teddy wasn't sure how Mr. Kane planned to change the Grid into a paradise, but if anyone could do it he knew Kane could.

Then Teddy reminded himself of why he had come to the Explorers Club that night and turned back to Commissioner Lynch. "About the murder, sir," he reminded the commissioner.

Commissioner Lynch shrugged. "This is the Grid," he said. "What's the surprise? According to the latest surveys, there's a crime every three minutes. But hourly polls show that the public quickly forgets them."

"No," insisted Teddy. "This was a dinocide."

A stunned look came over the commissioner's face. "A dinocide?" he asked with a start. "Now that *is* unusual!"

4

At that moment Deputy Commissioner Summers stepped over. "Sir, is something wrong?" he asked with concern.

"There's been a dinocide," Lynch told his deputy.

"Beg your pardon, sir," said Teddy. "But I'd like to be assigned to the case. As a detective."

Both commissioners stared at Teddy. His was a very unusual request. There had never been a dino-detective in the department before.

"You work in public relations, don't you, Teddy?" Commissioner Lynch asked.

"Yes," admitted Teddy. "But I joined the force to be a detective. I was trained to work the streets, not give Grid tours."

"But this crime calls for a pro," said Lynch. "A seasoned *Gun*."

■ 12 ■

"But your Guns are all human," said Teddy. "How do you expect them to solve a dino-murder?"

Lynch paused. Teddy had a good point.

Just then the butler walked over with a tray full of food.

"Sweets?" he offered Teddy and the others.

"Cookies!" Teddy exclaimed gleefully. "Yes!" Then he reached for a clawful.

"Just one per customer," insisted the butler.

Teddy frowned and took one cookie. Then, when the butler turned away, Teddy tapped him on the shoulder with his tail. Thinking it was someone else, the butler looked up, away from Teddy. That's when Teddy snuck another cookie off the butler's tray and began to gobble it down, macadamia cream filling first.

Deputy Summers pulled Commissioner Lynch aside. "Boss, this case of Teddy's is a hot one," he said in a wily tone of voice. "When news of this gets out, there could be riots."

"Riots?" asked Commissioner Lynch.

"Yes, sir," said Summers. "Dinosaurs on the rampage. Right now the press has wind that something's up. We've been able to hold them off for now, but we'll have to do something soon."

Commissioner Lynch quickly saw Summers's point. "A big-time crime could kill my law-and-order campaign for mayor," he concluded.

"What about our tall and shiny prince over

there?" Summers said pointing to Teddy, who was still busy gulping down his cookie. "We could make him our first dino-detective."

"Are you out of your mind?" asked Lynch.

"Track this with me, sir," said Summers. "Teddy solves the dinocide. Interspecies relations smooth over. Who's the hero?"

"Teddy Rex," said Commissioner Lynch.

"No," corrected Summers. "The hero is Lynch: the commissioner who had 'the vision to look beyond the species to save the town.' Forget being the next mayor. Think *Senator*."

Commissioner Lynch raised his eyebrows. "*Senator* Lynch?" he said. "It has a nice ring." Then, nodding knowingly to Summers, he approached Teddy.

"The case is yours, Teddy," he told the dinosaur. "You're undercover, no press, no fuss, just results by prime time tomorrow."

Teddy was so excited, his tail wagged up and down. "Thank you! Thank you! Thank you!" he told the commissioner.

"There's just one condition," added Lynch.

"There is?"

"We're teaming you up, for your own good," said Lynch. "With a veteran. A pro."

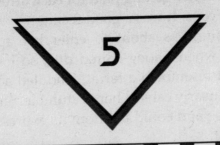

Katie Coltrane was still in her police uniform when she turned the corner and walked down the block toward her apartment house. She was tired, exhausted from her first day back on the job after three months on remotivation leave. The first day back was always the hardest. It was like a test. Just a few hours earlier she had been with Captain Alaric, her superior officer. They were on a stake-out in the deepest part of the Grid. Some scavengers, full-blooded clones known as Zapheads, were conducting some illegal gene smuggling. Coltrane broke up the deal and managed to arrest one of the Zapheads in the process. That was good enough for Alaric to give Coltrane the okay for reinstatement.

Now all Coltrane wanted was a good night's rest. Tomorrow she'd be back on the regular department roster getting paid for each arrest like all the other cops. It was a good feeling.

Coltrane was about to enter her apartment building when a long-haired dog, so low to the ground it resembled a ferret, waddled across her path and nearly caused her to stumble. She picked up the dog and could tell from its expression that it was lost.

"Just what I need," she told the sad-faced canine. "Another stray."

She carried the dog across the street and into a shabby-looking storefront with a worn sign that read EXOTIC FRUIT AND PROTEIN BAR over its entrance. A twelve-year-old boy behind the counter sat glued in front of a small holo-TV set on which a newscaster was announcing the latest statistics in the current rash of animals that were rapidly becoming extinct.

"Elephants, lions, whales. Now raccoons," the boy told Coltrane as she entered the shop. "Katie, what are grown-ups doing to the world?"

"Nothing we don't do to each other," Coltrane replied cynically. Then she held up the dachshund. "He yours, Sebastian?"

"My dad won't let me have a pet," replied Sebastian. "Anyway, looks like he's adopted *you*."

"Another stray," sighed Coltrane. "The word must be out on me."

"Well?"

"'Well' what?"

"How did your field test go?"

"I came through with flying colors," Coltrane replied proudly.

"Great!" Sebastian said.

Coltrane reached into her pocket and handed Sebastian a credit chip. "I'm feeling lucky," she said. "Gimme a lottery chip."

"Hey, you know the odds on winning the lottery?" asked Sebastian as he pressed a lever on a machine and pulled out a lottery ticket.

"I see. Only kids can dream?" Coltrane asked, taking the ticket. "Isn't it past your bedtime?"

"Naw. Dad said I could keep him company tonight. He'll be back any minute. He's lonely, Katie. Very lonely."

Coltrane could only groan. Sebastian had been relentlessly trying to fix her up with his dad ever since his mother had died three years before. Coltrane felt for the boy. She liked him. In fact, if she had to have a son she would want one just like him. But Coltrane didn't have room in her life for a family. Deep down she knew she never would.

"Can you swing by the bladegrounds tomorrow?" Sebastian asked.

"Not another blind date?"

"No. I promise."

Coltrane smiled and nodded at the boy. A game of Double Dog on blades might be just the thing after a day on the beat.

BEEEEEP! BEEEEEP!

Coltrane looked down. Her belt pager was beeping like crazy.

"Come in, Coltrane," came a voice over her buckle chip. It was the base operator.

Coltrane pressed a button on her buckle and answered: "Coltrane, on-line."

"Where are you?" asked the operator.

"Home. I'm off the clock."

"Not anymore," said the voice. "Report to the Explorers Club. The commissioner wants the pleasure of your company."

"The commissioner?" Coltrane asked in disbelief. "He wants *me*?"

"Yes," replied the base operator. "The order is logged on the emergency frequency. Coltrane to Explorers Club. Now go."

"Well," sighed Coltrane, realizing at once that her good night's rest would have to wait. "He itches and we scratch."

Coltrane was escorted to the Explorers Club in a squad car. She arrived just as Commissioner Lynch, Deputy Summers, and Teddy were emerging from the club.

"There's been a homicide and your name came up," Deputy Summers told Coltrane.

"Actually, it's a dinocide," interrupted Teddy. "A dinosaur is dead."

"Like *extinct*?" asked Coltrane.

"Like murdered," replied Teddy.

Coltrane's eyebrows lifted. "That's a first," she said.

"Katie Coltrane, meet Teddy Rex," Commissioner Lynch said, introducing the two. "Teddy's in public relations, but I'm field-promoting him temporarily. You two solve this case together."

Coltrane looked at Lynch as if he had just lost his mind. "What? Me teamed up with a dino?" she asked doubtfully. "Suppose something goes wrong? I'm no dino-sitter."

"He graduated from the academy just like you did," Summers told her.

"So what am I?" Coltrane shot back. "An extension course? Teddy's a house-mouse at headquarters. I'll be the laughingstock of the department!"

"Get me results by prime time tomorrow," Commissioner Lynch told Coltrane, "and I'll double your regular commission. The official log will show this is not a request!"

And with that the commissioner strode down the steps, climbed into his waiting limo, and drove off.

"Suits," Coltrane grunted resentfully. "I can't stand suits."

Summers leaned over. "If you don't fly straight," he warned Coltrane, "you'll be back on remotivation leave. This is your comeback shot. Don't miss the boat." Then he turned around and walked away.

Alone together for the first time, Teddy and Coltrane stared uncomfortably at each other for a long moment. Coltrane stared up. Teddy stared down.

"Just what exactly do you do in public relations?" Coltrane asked Teddy.

"I give city tours to visiting dignitaries," replied Teddy.

Coltrane groaned, "I'm working with a *tour guide*?"

"Hey, look," said Teddy. "As long as we're partners, why not make the best of it?"

Don't use that word," insisted Coltrane.

"What word?" asked Teddy.

"*Partners!*" retorted Coltrane. "We're not partners. We're not pals. This is a shotgun wedding."

Later that evening Deputy Summers left the Explorers Club and climbed into a waiting limousine. Inside were Elizar Kane and Dr. Shade.

"This dinocide thing could blow up in our faces," Summers said as the limo started off. "But I took care of it."

"Thank you, Alex," said Mr. Kane. "Exactly how did you do this?"

"I made the commissioner assign the case to the department's token dino."

"A dino for a dino case," Dr. Shade said in a skeptical tone of voice.

"I teamed up that little scale Teddy Rex with Coltrane from Gun Command," continued Summers. "She's just back from remotivation leave."

"Remotivation leave?" asked Dr. Shade.

"She was sent there because she was on the slide," explained Summers.

"So it's a case of the blind leading the blind," said Mr. Kane.

"They'll never connect the dots back to you, sir," Summers assured Mr. Kane. "They fail and we succeed. This is where I get out."

The limo stopped and Deputy Summers got out. When he was gone, Dr. Shade pressed a button and the partition window separating the backseats from the front ones zipped down. Sitting beside the driver was a large, broad-shouldered man with a jaw like granite and a pair of sunglasses that hid his eyes.

"Maybe we should get rid of Teddy Rex," Dr. Shade suggested to the man.

"Don't worry about him," said the man. "A scale detective is a sideshow."

"Don't be so sure, Edge," said Mr. Kane. "Our little dino is intelligent, honest, and loyal. He's more concerned with justice than any softskin money can buy. And with Coltrane, things could spiral out of control."

"Coltrane," Edge repeated the name as if he'd heard it somewhere before.

"You know the name?" asked Mr. Kane.

"Ten years ago she intercepted and freeze-dried our best genetic code smuggler," said Edge.

"Now I remember," said Kane. "She cost us a fortune."

"We put our best Flame Team on her," said Edge.

"And your best wasn't good enough," added Dr. Shade.

Edge smiled. "She was lucky," he said with bitterness. "Tell me what you want to happen."

"Just have them followed," said Kane. "I don't want anyone to sense our concern. And Edge, you know how I feel about failure. It reeks of imperfection. Another setback and I will hold you personally responsible."

"What's wrong?" Teddy asked as he waited for Coltrane to get into the Rex Cruiser.

"I don't want anyone to see me in this," replied Coltrane as she climbed in. She looked silly sitting in the oversized seat.

"Seat belts," said Teddy.

"Seat belts?"

"Safety first."

Coltrane fastened her huge seat belt. It felt very uncomfortable.

"I can raise your seat if you like," offered Teddy.

"No," insisted Coltrane. "Don't."

But it was too late. Teddy pulled a lever and Coltrane's seat shot straight up. *CRASH!* She hit the roof so hard, she became pinned to the top.

"Sorry," said Teddy. "I'll lower you."

"No!" said Coltrane. "Don't touch anything. I'll do it myself!"

And with that Coltrane reached down and pushed the seat lever forward. *CRASH!* The seat plunged to the floor.

"It's a pleasure to work with a professional," said Teddy.

"Crash it, lizard lips," said Coltrane as she rubbed her sore back. "This isn't one of your tours!"

"Whatever you say," said Teddy.

"I'm scared to ask," Coltrane said. "What's next?"

"Well, let's see," replied Teddy thoughtfully. "This is a homicide."

"Very good," Coltrane said sarcastically.

"The investigator goes back to the beginning and back to the body!"

"Right," agreed Coltrane. "But there's never been a dinocide before. Where would they do a dino-autopsy?"

"I got it!" exclaimed Teddy. Then he stepped on the gas pedal and screeched the Rex Cruiser across town, stopping a few minutes later in front of the Natural History Museum.

Once inside, Teddy and Coltrane were directed through the Hall of Reptiles to the dinosaurology lab. It was there they would find the body of the murdered dino.

Teddy sighed balefully as he and Coltrane

moved through the Hall of Reptiles and saw the displays of ancient dinosaur skeletons.

"Museums give me the blues," he said sadly.

"Why's that?" asked Coltrane.

"It's like I feel my ancestors looking down at me from across time."

"Yeah? And what do they say?"

"They want me to do the best I can," said Teddy. "Give it one hundred percent."

Coltrane rolled her eyes.

"Don't you have a guardian angel?" Teddy asked Coltrane.

"Yeah. Me," Coltrane replied flatly.

"Well," said Teddy. "I keep hoping your species will wake up before you become extinct like everything else around here."

"I just keep hoping I'll wake up from this case," replied Coltrane with a groan.

They passed through a doorway framed by the jaws of a huge prehistoric shark and entered a room with a lot of laboratory equipment inside. In the center of the room was a huge table. On the table, illuminated by a battery of work lights, was the dino that Teddy had seen in his flash.

"Do you know him?" Coltrane asked Teddy.

"No," said Teddy. "You?"

"Hey, all dinos look the same to me," replied Coltrane.

Just then a woman in a white laboratory coat

and wire-rimmed spectacles emerged from an inner office.

"Who are you two?" asked the woman with an annoyed tone. She obviously didn't like intruders. "Let's see some ID."

Coltrane held up her badge.

"Grid Police Gun Command," said Coltrane. "Who're *you*?"

"Dr. Leila Amitraj," said the woman. "Head dinosaurologist, Grid Natural History Museum. What can I do for you?"

"We're investigating this dinocide," said Teddy, pointing to the dino on the table.

Dr. Amitraj threw a surprised look at Teddy. "You?" she asked. "You're a detective?"

"Yes," Teddy replied proudly.

"*Temporarily*," added Coltrane.

"That's too bad," said Dr. Amitraj. "Dinos have hearts and souls. Things we humans just pretend we have."

"Can we move this along?" Coltrane asked insistently.

"Right," said the dinosaurologist. "This dino died from an explosion close to the snout. I took a look and couldn't find any concrete evidence."

"Hmmm," said Teddy. "Let me have a peek." Then he leaned in for a closer look at the dead dino. Grabbing a pair of tweezers from the instrument table, he plucked a small metal flake from its snout. "Doctor Amitraj," he said, handing the flake to the dinosaurologist, "send this to the lab. Maybe they can reconstruct whatever it was. And run metallurgy and spectrum tests. Now for the prints."

"Fingerprints?" asked Coltrane.

"No," replied Teddy. "We dinos don't have fingerprints. The scale patterns on our tails are all different."

Teddy took the victim's tail, dipped it in a small jar of special ink, and made a triangular tailprint on a piece of paper. Then he went over to Dr. Amitraj's computer terminal and punched in his access code.

"You've reached Teddy Rex's home," came a voice over the computer. It was Chip, Teddy's home computer. "How can I help you?"

"Hello, Chip. This is Teddy. I need an ID on this tailprint."

Teddy fed the piece of paper with the print on it into the computer.

"ID completed and verified," said Chip after a few busy *whirrs* and *buzzes*. "Oliver Rex, unemployed, resides at thirty-five Prehistoric Place with Molly Rex. End file."

"Molly Rex," Teddy said as if he recognized the name.

"You know her?" Coltrane asked.

"I wish I did," replied Teddy wistfully. "She sings at the local club." Then Teddy turned to Dr.

Amitraj and said: "Good night, doc. Sorry to barge in."

Coltrane thought that was a little bit *too* polite. "Hey, why not do the doc's laundry while you're at it?" she quipped as she and Teddy left the laboratory.

"Do you fight with *everyone*?" asked Teddy.

"Since we're working together, let's get the ground rules straight," Coltrane shot back. "We're on a case. *We* ask questions. *They* answer. Or else."

"People might help you more if you treated them with respect," Teddy gently suggested.

"In the Grid, if they fear you, they respect you," insisted Coltrane. "And you might stay vertical."

"But it's nice to be nice," Teddy insisted back.

"What are you? A fortune cookie?"

"No," said Teddy. "But I'm polite."

"It's going to be a long night," Coltrane said, rolling her eyes for the second time that evening. "Where now?"

"We have a talk with Molly Rex."

8

"Ewww, what's that smell?" Coltrane asked, covering her nose.

"Clean air," answered Teddy, taking a deep breath of purified air.

They had just entered the Extinct Species Club and all around them the place was jumping with activity. Guests of the club—dinosaurs of all different species—were sitting at tables, eating and drinking. Dinosaur waiters and waitresses were ushering guests to tables and taking their orders. A dino-comedian stood on the stage, finishing up his act to much laughter and applause.

A waitress guided Teddy and Coltrane to a table near the stage. Teddy ordered a glacier water and Coltrane ordered a glass of unfiltered Grid brown. Then Teddy pressed a button on the table and a bubbling bowl of greenish brown liquid emerged through the tabletop.

"This is dinner?" asked Coltrane.

"They're hydroponic greens and krill," explained Teddy. "All grown naturally, no chemicals. Snarf up." Grabbing a floating water lily, Teddy scooped up some of the soup and sucked it down.

Coltrane watched, disgusted. "I thought your crowd were meat eaters," she said. "Bronto-burgers and Stego-steaks. Beat 'em and eat 'em."

"We were, originally," replied Teddy. "But ever since we were brought back from extinction we've been strictly vegetarian. You humans should give it a try."

Skeptically Coltrane picked up a strand of food and took a careful bite, gagging as she tried to swallow. Just then the lights dimmed and a spotlight fell across the stage. The stage curtains parted and a beautiful dinosauress emerged. She wore several feather boas around her neck, a tight-fitting sequin gown that parted just at the tail, and a tiara. She also had the longest eyelashes that Teddy had ever seen.

Teddy and Coltrane knew at once that this was Molly Rex, the main attraction at the Extinct Species Club. After some eager applause from the audience, Molly began to sing. Her voice was so warm and sultry that Teddy could not take his eyes off her.

"I can't stop thinking about Oliver Rex," Teddy said to Coltrane as he watched Molly.

"Life is tough," said Coltrane.

"Hey," said Teddy. "Try being dropped into a world sixty-five million years past your prime."

"Look, Teddy, it's not easy even if this is your time."

"Yeah," said Teddy reflectively. "Maybe the old days weren't so sweet, either."

"What old days?"

"Herds of duckbills grazing on the plains, brontosaurus on the riverbanks, pterodactyls in the sky."

"And T-Rexes munching out on everybody," Coltrane added sharply.

"Still, it must have felt like one big family," Teddy said wistfully.

"If it's a family you want," Coltrane said, "ask for the recipe and hatch yourself a few brothers and sisters."

Just then Molly Rex finished her song. The audience burst into wild applause, with Teddy clapping the loudest.

"Brava . . . brava!" Teddy shouted as Molly took several bows and walked offstage. Teddy grabbed a floral arrangement from his table, wrapped it in a napkin like a bouquet, and followed Molly.

"That girl-osaurus is trouble," Coltrane told herself. Then she got up and trailed the lovestruck dino-detective backstage.

9

BACKSTAGE, MIDNIGHT

Teddy stood in the doorway of the dressing room for a long time, watching Molly Rex as she sat at her vanity and removed her stage makeup. Then, when he thought the moment was right, he stepped inside and handed the beautiful singer the bouquet he had made for her.

"Have we met?" Molly asked Teddy.

"My partner and I, or is it *me*, saw your act," Teddy replied, slightly nervous.

"Partner?" asked Molly. She looked over and saw Coltrane, who had just arrived at the dressing room door.

"Grid Police," said Coltrane, introducing herself.

"I took you for talent agents," said Molly, sounding slightly disappointed.

"Your voice is wonderful," Teddy told Molly.

"Why, yes, it is," said Molly, blushing.

Coltrane cleared her throat. "Look, we're not here for autographs," she said, trying to get down to business.

"Something terrible is up," Molly told the detectives.

"What makes you say that?" asked Coltrane.

"Because last night I was dead asleep, and out of nowhere I got this *flash* — "

"Me too!" Teddy exclaimed.

"Of course," said Molly. She and Teddy stared into each other's eyes as if they shared a special secret. "When dinos connect, words aren't important," Molly said.

"Yeah, only grunts," interrupted Coltrane. "Look, we're after a killer."

"You're after a killer?" Molly asked. Now she was surprised.

"The murderer of Oliver Rex," explained Coltrane.

Molly paused and stopped removing makeup from her face. Teddy could see that she was upset.

"Ollie . . . is dead?" she asked quietly.

Teddy nodded and waited patiently for her to recover from the shock.

"What did Oliver do for a living?" Coltrane asked Molly.

"He entertained at kids' birthday parties, and worked at theme parks and conventions," Molly replied.

"That's it?"

"Well, actually," Molly continued, "Oliver was a New Eden volunteer. He said it was Earth's only hope."

"New Eden?" asked Coltrane.

"Miss Rex," Teddy said, handing Molly his card, "if you think of anything else, here's my number."

Molly took Teddy's card and placed it on her vanity.

"I know it won't bring your friend back, but I feel for you," said Teddy.

"What a sweet thing to say," said Molly. "By the way, what sign are you, Mr. Rex?"

"Mesozoic," answered Teddy. "Call me Teddy."

"I'll call you Theo," said Molly. "My friends call me Molly."

"Mine just call me collect," said Coltrane. And with that she grabbed Teddy by the arm and pulled him through the door so hard he bumped his head on its frame on the way out.

But Teddy was so thrilled at having met Molly Rex that he didn't feel a thing.

THE REX CRUISER, 12:29 A.M.

No sooner had they emerged from the nightclub than Coltrane's belt beeper began to flash red. She was needed at headquarters.

"Where to?" asked Teddy as they reached the Rex Cruiser.

"For you, it's beddy-bye," Coltrane told Teddy.

"What?"

"Go home, get some sleep. We'll pick up the trail in the morning."

"But — "

Coltrane held up her belt beeper. "Keep your homing beeper linked to mine and don't argue," she said. "Go!"

Teddy held up his beeper and set it for Coltrane's frequency. "Buzz if you need me," he told her.

"Sure," said Coltrane. Then she walked away.

Teddy watched as Coltrane disappeared down the street. Then he climbed into the Rex Cruiser and switched on the ignition. Teddy put the cruiser into reverse . . . and backed into the car behind him.

Just as Teddy was starting to pull out, four thugs dressed in hooded sweatshirts and baggy jeans converged on the Rex Cruiser.

"Hey, you kids!" shouted Teddy. "This is an official police vehicle!"

But the thugs paid no attention to Teddy's plea. Instead, they beat the Rex Cruiser with chains, snapped off its door panels, and crashed in its roof.

Teddy screamed. He knew he was in trouble and needed help. Instinctively he reached down and pressed the button on his homing beeper.

Meanwhile, the thugs continued to trash the Rex Cruiser. They pulled off its wheels and sent them rolling down the street. They smashed in its windows. They even removed the engine and exploded it into a huge fireball.

BANG! BANG! BANG! Suddenly a shower of bullets landed all around the thugs. When Teddy looked up he saw a gun-toting figure emerge through the smoke and fire and come straight toward him on motorized Rollerblades.

Teddy felt himself sigh with relief when he recognized the figure who had come to his rescue. It was Coltrane.

Before Coltrane could fire again the thugs fled, knocking into each other as they did so. When she was sure Teddy was safe Coltrane came to a stop, put her gun away, and helped Teddy squeeze himself out of the crushed cruiser.

"I thought I told you to go straight home!" she scolded him.

"I was, but — " Teddy started to explain.

"Zapheads!" said Coltrane.

"Zapheads?" asked Teddy. He had never heard the term before.

"That's who those freaks were," explained Coltrane. "Low IQ's and high pain thresholds. Why didn't you pull your gun?"

"What gun?" asked Teddy. He never carried a weapon.

"You're unarmed?!"

Teddy nodded. "Actually, I don't believe in violence," he said proudly.

"You must lead a charmed life," said Coltrane in disbelief.

"Can't you tell?" asked Teddy.

Teddy pulled a fire extinguisher from the cruiser.

Coltrane suddenly became angry. "Stay alert!" she said in a reprimanding tone. "Stay alive! I told you this wasn't a game!"

Teddy switched on the fire extinguisher and doused the smoldering cruiser with foam. A smile had come to his face. Despite some of the mean things she had said to him in the past, Coltrane had saved his life. That could only mean one thing, he realized happily: She cared.

POLICE HEADQUARTERS, 9:29 A.M.

The following morning Teddy and Coltrane arrived at Police Headquarters and immediately put in a request for a new Rex-friendly cruiser.

"I've got the perfect vehicle for you two!" said the desk officer with a giggle. Then he punched an order for a new cruiser into the computer.

After a few minutes Teddy and Coltrane noticed that some of the other officers were staring at them.

A few were even trying to suppress snickers at the sight of the big dino and the little Gun.

Coltrane rolled her eyes, embarrassed. She didn't like being laughed at.

They were on their way to give their report to Commissioner Lynch when the elevator doors opened and Deputy Summers stepped out.

"Well?" Summers asked. "Where are the fruits of your labor last night?"

"I was attacked, Mr. Summers," said Teddy as he pointed to a black-and-blue bump on his head.

"The reports say your vehicle was stripped," said Summers. "With you in it."

"Someone put a Flame Team on him," explained Coltrane.

"Obviously someone's scared we're on the case," suggested Teddy.

"I know the commissioner is," Summers remarked snippily.

A stern expression came over Coltrane's face. "I told you and the commissioner this team-up idea was way off!" she exclaimed.

"Coltrane," began Summers, "be the solution, not the problem for a change, okay?" And with that he walked away.

Teddy could tell that Coltrane was upset at the remark. He knew, after all, that this was her first case back on the job and she didn't want to blow it.

"You okay, Katie?" he asked her.

Coltrane started up the stairs. "I'm working with a talking dinosaur on a hopeless case for morons," she replied with a groan. "I'm *peachy*!"

"We'll come through, I know we will," Teddy said as they emerged on the second floor a minute later.

"'*We*'?" Coltrane snapped back. "We're not a

'*we.*' We're not a team, partners, or anything. We're a cop blind date!"

Teddy frowned. "I'm sorry," he said in a hurt tone of voice.

"*Stop apologizing!*" exclaimed Coltrane in frustration.

"Sorry," said Teddy.

"*Stop!*" said Coltrane.

Just then an office door opened and Commissioner Lynch stepped out.

"Teddy," he said upon seeing the big dino. "Your tour car was bought with taxpayers' money. You've been on the case for twelve hours and you've got zip to show for it. We cut a deal, Teddy. You wanted the case, I wanted a boost in my polls, not *two* dead dinos!"

"And *I* didn't want this case," Coltrane said.

Now Lynch turned to Katie Coltrane. "Coltrane, you embarrassed the department."

"Sir," Teddy interrupted. "It was I who let the department down, not Katie."

Coltrane looked at Teddy, surprised that he was sticking up for her.

"You don't know enough to take the blame for this," Commissioner Lynch told Teddy.

"Sir, the dino has potential," Coltrane said, jumping in to defend Teddy. "He knows his stuff."

Lynch just rolled his eyes. "A Gun and a dinosaur detective! This was Summers's idea!" he

wailed. "I know: I'll blame *him*. That's what em-
ployees are for!"

"You mean Laserhead stuck us together?"
Coltrane asked suspiciously. She knew how little
Deputy Summers thought of her.

"That's right," replied the commissioner. "He
said you were the one for the job. Said you still
had the magic. Remember, this case better be gift-
wrapped by prime time tonight — or *else!*"

And with that order Commissioner Lynch
spun around and walked away. When they were
alone, Coltrane turned to Teddy.

"Hey!" she said.

Teddy jumped back. "What did I do now?" he
asked, cowering.

"Back there," began Coltrane in a voice that almost sounded pleasant. "You told Lynch that I'm
on top of things."

"That's right."

"Well, no one ever stuck up for me before,"
Coltrane said softly. Then one side of her mouth
turned upward into a half-smile, which Teddy realized was better than no smile at all.

Next Coltrane took a long look at Teddy's
clothes. They were in tatters from the attack the
night before. She motioned for him to follow her,
then led him into a room marked SUPPLIES. A po-
licewoman was sitting behind the supply desk,
putting on a whole new shade of computerized

lipstick when she looked up and saw Coltrane and Teddy.

"Hi, Ella," Coltrane greeted the supply officer.

Ella looked Coltrane up and down and whistled. "Girlfriend," she said, "you look like I feel."

"I feel like I look," said Coltrane. "Teddy, say hello to Ella."

"Pleased to meet you," Teddy said.

"Charmed," replied Ella.

"Teddy's here to be a chic scale," Coltrane said.

Ella got the idea immediately and pulled out her tape measure.

"Something inconspicuous," requested Teddy.

"Make him blend," said Coltrane.

"Try the zoo," Ella replied. Then she went to work. She placed Teddy on a holograph pad and entered some choices into a computer. One by one, Teddy appeared in a variety of laser-imaged outfits as Coltrane and Ella searched for the perfect fit. There was a Western look, complete with neckerchief and lasso. There was metal-plated medieval knight's armor, nearly perfect for a dino-investigator on the go. There were even the swashbuckling sashes and swords of a pirate.

Finally a pair of jeans, an orange hooded sweatshirt, brown leather jacket, and high-top sneakers appeared on Teddy. They made him look like a true plainclothes detective!

"I look like a real cop!" Teddy exclaimed happily as he stepped off the holograph platform.

"Don't let it throw you," cautioned Coltrane. "Where to now?"

"New Eden," Teddy said with certainty.

"New Eden?"

Teddy explained: "Molly said Oliver was a New Eden volunteer, remember?"

"What about it?" Coltrane sounded hesitant. Elizar Kane was in charge of New Eden and he was a pretty powerful person.

"You don't want to go there?" Teddy asked with some surprise.

"I'll go anywhere to solve a case," replied Coltrane. "But, Teddy, Elizar Kane eats billionaires for breakfast."

"Good for him," Teddy said, undaunted.

"You want to tie the richest man in the Grid to murder?" Coltrane asked.

"Remember what you once told me," Teddy reminded the Gun as they headed out to claim their new cruiser. "'We're on a case. We ask, they answer.'"

"I don't have to take that from a reptile," said Coltrane, although secretly she had to admit that Teddy was absolutely right.

The new Rex Cruiser wasn't exactly the perfect vehicle. Instead, it was a police department garbage truck with the name COLTRANE posted on its side on a piece of cardboard from an old pizza carton. Anyone who saw it laughed out loud as it lumbered through the Grid side streets and slowly approached an alley. Coltrane was driving the truck and Teddy was sitting beside her. Both were cowering with embarrassment.

A group of kids on Rollerblades was playing a game of alley hockey as Coltrane approached and brought the truck to a stop. One of the kids was Sebastian.

"Nice blading," Coltrane told Sebastian as she and Teddy climbed out of the truck.

"What are you talking about?" replied Sebastian with a tone of disappointment as he skated over to them. "You just rolled in."

Coltrane felt bad. She knew she had promised to meet Sebastian for the game. She didn't like breaking promises to him. "It's the thought that counts," she said, apologizing.

"Hey, stick around," said Sebastian. "My dad's coming. My lonely widower dad."

"Didn't I say stop matchmaking?" Coltrane asked with a laugh.

Sebastian smiled, obviously forgiving her absence. Then he pulled a small gift-wrapped object out of his pocket and handed it to her. "No strings," he told her.

Coltrane opened the gift. It was a leather wallet with her initials on it. "It's beautiful," she said.

"It's a badge case," explained Sebastian. "Now that you're a Gun again. I finished it this morning."

"These Grid kids are smooth," said Teddy, who had been watching Sebastian's friends as they played hockey.

"He with you?" Sebastian asked Coltrane.

"Sebastian," said Coltrane, "meet Theodore Rex."

"They partnered you with a dinosaur?" Sebastian asked with astonishment.

"He's not my partner," insisted Coltrane. "He's more like my — "

"*Associate, friend,*" Teddy cut in. "You're good on wheels, Sebastian."

"Thanks," said Sebastian. "Do you blade?"

"A little," replied Teddy. "How about you, Katie?"

"Hey, I'm a Grid kid," said Coltrane. "I grew up on war wheels."

Upon hearing this, Sebastian and his friends gathered around the two detectives and began chanting: "Shoot-out! Shoot-out!" They wanted to see a match between Coltrane and Teddy.

Coltrane took a hockey stick from Sebastian while one of the other kids lined up six street-hockey balls across from the goal. Sebastian tended goal. Then Coltrane leaned in and made a swipe at each of the pucks. She made three easy goals. The kids cheered.

"Here," Coltrane said, handing the hockey stick to Teddy. "You're on-line. Beat that."

Teddy rolled up his sleeves as the kids lined up the balls again. Sebastian hunched in front of the goal net, waiting for Teddy to begin.

Suddenly Teddy angled the end of his tail as if it were a hockey stick. Then he swiftly began swatting the balls with his tail. *WAP! SWIPE! SWAT! SWOOSH! WAP! PING!* He smashed the balls across the alley and past Sebastian, making six easy goals.

When he was done, he raised the tip of his tail

to his lips and blew across it as if he were a gun-fighter cooling off his six-shooter after a shoot-out.

Even Coltrane was impressed, although she tried her best not to show it. Instead, she pulled Teddy to the side and showed him her watch. It was time to get back to work.

It was time to visit New Eden.

It was a long drive to New Eden. The compound sat several miles away in an area outside the Grid that Teddy and Coltrane had heard of, but had never seen. As soon as they arrived they were met by a guard in a jeep. They parked their garbage truck and climbed into the jeep. Then they were driven through a tall gate.

The New Eden compound was not like the Grid at all. There were no dense metal buildings closely packed together in a maze of interconnecting rows. There were hardly even any people.

New Eden was a park. Its gates opened up on a lush, sprawling vista of green hills and forests. As Teddy and Coltrane were driven through the grounds they passed herds of zebra, elephants, lions, giraffes, and rhinos.

In the center of everything was a huge building with high columns and tall windows that reflected the bright sunlight. The jeep came to a stop in front of the building and let Teddy and Coltrane out. Another guard emerged from the building and led them inside and upstairs to a special waiting room. After a few moments Dr. Shade entered the room. She seemed surprised to see Teddy.

"Welcome to New Eden, Mr. Rex," she said.

"Thank you," said Teddy.

"We're here to see Mr. Kane," said Coltrane rather abruptly.

"I see," said Dr. Shade. "He is a busy man."

"I'm Coltrane. Gun Command," Katie said.

"Of course," said Dr. Shade, clearly sensing the importance of the visit. "I'm Dr. Shade, Mr. Kane's personal physician. Follow me."

Teddy and Coltrane followed Dr. Shade down the hall and into a large office that was filled with expensive-looking furniture and laboratory equipment. A man was hunched over one of the lab tables. As soon as they entered the room the man looked up. Teddy recognized him immediately. It was Elizar Kane.

"Hello, again, Theodore," Mr. Kane said, greeting Teddy.

"Hi, Mr. Kane," said Teddy. "I'd like you to meet my — "

But Coltrane reached out and shook Mr. Kane's hand before Teddy could finish. "Hello," she said coolly. "Coltrane. Gun Command."

Teddy was embarrassed. "We're sorry to disturb you, sir," he said.

"Do you have a second?" asked Mr. Kane, not seeming to mind the intrusion. "I've something wonderful to show you."

Teddy and Coltrane joined Mr. Kane at the lab table. A large fish tank sat on the table. In it were several small silver fish that seemed to glitter in the light.

"Are you familiar with ice fish?" asked Mr. Kane.

"No," replied Teddy.

Kane pressed a button on the table. All at once the water in the fish tank turned into a solid block of ice. The fish became frozen inside.

Teddy and Coltrane stared with wide-eyed astonishment at the sight.

"Remarkable creatures," said Mr. Kane. "They live in our polar oceans, in water so cold no other organisms can survive."

"But how?" asked Teddy.

"They possess an enzyme, which I have isolated and reproduced," explained Kane. "It is the key to their survival. Because of it ice fish can be trapped frozen in ice for years and then brought back to life."

Kane pressed another button on the lab table. This time the ice melted back into water and the silver fish inside began to swim freely about as if nothing had happened.

"Suspended animation," observed Coltrane.

"Wow!" exclaimed Teddy with amazement.

"Yes," said Kane. "After injecting the serum taken from the ice fish into a subject's blood, they can be frozen and brought back to life—whenever."

"This isn't a social call," Coltrane said, abruptly changing the subject. "We're here because somebody gave Oliver Rex a new cosmic address."

"No need to take an attitude, officer," said Dr. Shade, who was standing behind them. "How can we help you?"

"We're here investigating a dinocide," explained Teddy.

"Oliver?" uttered Mr. Kane. He sounded surprised.

"You knew him?" asked Coltrane.

"Of course," admitted Kane.

"Did he have any enemies that you knew of?" asked Teddy.

"I can't imagine Oliver making a single enemy," replied Mr. Kane.

"It just takes one . . ." Coltrane said, thinking aloud.

Teddy and Coltrane had finished asking their questions. They were about to leave when Coltrane caught sight of a large drawing on the wall. It looked like a picture of a giant honeycomb. The words SPECIES DATA were written across the top of the drawing.

"What is 'Species Data'?" Coltrane asked Mr. Kane with curiosity.

"My foundation tracks vanishing life-forms," explained Mr. Kane. "We try to rescue the last specimens, when we can, and keep them here at the compound. We keep records of vanishing animal species."

Teddy reached out his tail and shook Mr. Kane's hand good-bye. Then he and Coltrane left.

When they had gone, a troubled look came over Kane's face. "This is getting out of hand," he told Dr. Shade.

"They are fools," replied Dr. Shade.

"Luck favors fools," said Kane. "The Rex is a child. Harmless, maybe. But, Coltrane is street smart."

"According to Summers, she's lost her touch."

Just then the door opened and Edge entered. He pulled a small holo-video disk out of his pocket and placed it in front of Kane.

"What's this?" asked Kane.

"Insurance," sneered Edge. He slipped the disc into a holo-player and touched a button. A holographic image of Coltrane and Sebastian playing hockey in the alley appeared before them.

Kane understood immediately and smiled. That's when he gave Edge a new order: Kidnap Sebastian.

Teddy and Coltrane waited politely as the mourners filed out of the chapel where Oliver Rex's body had been recycled. It was Teddy's idea to go to the recycling ceremony and Coltrane thought it was a good one. Here they could question Oliver's friends, neighbors, and acquaintances. They were looking for a clue, a lead, anything.

But it was Molly Rex whom Teddy was most interested in. He hadn't been able to get the beautiful dinosauress out of his thoughts since the night he first saw her at the Extinct Species Club. Even though he hardly knew her he knew he cared for her.

"Molly?" Teddy asked politely as she emerged from the chapel.

"*Oui*, Teddy?" replied Molly. Despite the sad

circumstances the sight of Teddy seemed to cheer her.

"Once again, I'm so sorry about Oliver," Teddy said gently. "If there's anything I can do . . ."

"How gallant," Molly said, looking into Teddy's eyes warmly. "Would a walk home be too much?"

"Much too much," interrupted Coltrane, trying to pull Teddy away from Molly.

Teddy smiled. A walk with Molly was an invitation he couldn't turn down. Taking her arm, Teddy guided her off down the street.

Coltrane was left to follow along behind.

"I'm sorry we met under these circumstances," said Teddy after he and Molly had begun walking.

"Me, too," agreed Molly. "But I suppose it proves every cloud has a silver lining."

Teddy paused. He was feeling very shy. After a few quiet seconds he said quite timidly, "Er . . . Molly, I was wondering — ?"

"Yes, Theo?"

"Well . . . I mean . . . would you like to go out with me for krill sometime?"

"Gee, I don't think so," replied Molly.

"Oh," Teddy said sadly. He felt his heart sink. It was the one opportunity he had to ask Molly out and he had blown it.

But then Molly quickly added, "Seafood disagrees with me, but I'm a fool for macadamia chip cookies."

Suddenly Teddy cheered up. He had just

baked a batch of macadamia chip cookies the other day and he happily told Molly so.

"Homemade cookies?" asked Molly.

"From scratch," answered Teddy. "You take two cups of chips, one cup of flour, and lots of sugar!"

"How could I say no to a Rex who bakes cookies from scratch?"

A big grin came over Teddy's face. He cheerfully led Molly the few short blocks to his apartment.

Coltrane had tired of tagging along after the two starry-eyed Rexes. Rolling her eyes once more and shaking her head, she gave up and headed back to the garbage truck instead.

By now Molly and Teddy had entered his building. "I'm sorry the place is such a mess," Teddy said apologetically as he opened the door to his apartment and led Molly inside.

Molly saw that Teddy had exaggerated. His apartment was hardly a mess. In fact, with its freshly trimmed potted plants and cheerful orange-and-aqua color scheme, Molly thought that the apartment was positively immaculate (for a male Rex, that is).

"It's so . . . cozy," Molly said politely.

Almost as soon as they entered, Zippy ambled over and stood in front of them, his tongue panting.

"What's his name?" Molly asked as she bent

over to pat the dog on the head. But Zippy ignored her and walked away.

"Zippy! Don't be rude!" Teddy scolded the little dog. Then he had to explain to Molly: "He's sad because I left him alone last night."

"It's hard to be alone," Molly said sympathetically.

"I know," agreed Teddy. He could tell that Molly was still upset about losing her friend Oliver. He moved a step closer to her.

The two dinosaurs looked into each other's eyes.

"Theo?" asked Molly.

"Yes, Molly?" replied Teddy.

But Molly didn't say anything. Instead she moved a step closer to Teddy. Then, without saying a word, she gently wrapped her tail around his.

Being with him like this, Molly didn't feel so lonely anymore.

Sebastian was feeling great. His team had won the alley hockey game with a fourteen-point shutout. Now he was heading home, skating along the streets of the Grid with a big smile across his face.

He was no more than a block away from home when he heard strange sounds coming from the alleyway next to his building. As he got closer he recognized the sounds as a series of electronic *beeps* and *whirrs*, the kind you might hear coming from a holo-video game.

Sebastian turned down the opening to the alley and came to a stop. Indeed, at the far end of the alley a kid in a hooded sweatshirt was standing on a milk crate hunched over a video game.

Curious, Sebastian slowly skated forward and watched with fascination as the hooded kid made score after score as he played the game. No sooner had he begun his approach than the hooded kid finished his game, jumped off the milk crate, and ran out of the alley.

Sebastian excitedly dropped his backpack and climbed up on the milk crate. Then he switched on the game.

But nothing happened. No *beeps*. No *whirrs*. No *nothing*.

Sebastian tried to turn the game on a second time. Again nothing happened.

Then all of a sudden two clawlike clamps popped out from the sides of the video game and grabbed Sebastian by his wrists. Sebastian was surprised. Helpless, he felt himself being pulled forward, video game and all, into an opening in the alley wall.

Only it wasn't a wall at all. It was the back doors of a truck disguised to *look* like a wall. Without warning, the doors of the truck closed behind him. All around him was total darkness. The next thing he knew, he could hear the engine of the truck start up and feel himself being driven away.

16

Teddy and Molly spent the rest of the afternoon popping macadamia chip cookies into their mouths from the cookie shooter and talking. They talked about everything: where they were hatched, who their favorite dino movie stars were, where their favorite beach to go scale-bathing was. After a while Teddy put on a music CD of his favorite *stomp-and-roll* group, *The Paleolithic Fossils*. Then he and Molly danced.

"You're a wonderful dancer," Teddy told Molly as they stomped around the room.

"You must have swept a lot of girls off their feet," said Molly.

"No," replied Teddy red-faced. He was embarrassed to admit that he had never had a steady, regular reptile girlfriend.

After a moment Teddy stopped dancing. "I can't describe what I'm feeling," he told Molly.

"You don't have to," Molly said warmly. "The best things can't be told, only felt."

BEEP! BEEP! BEEP! Teddy's belt beeper started beeping like mad. Teddy knew it was Coltrane trying to reach him and that it was time for him to go.

"I'd like you to wear this," he told Molly. Then he took a ring off one of his three toes and placed it on one of Molly's.

"Your police ring," Molly said.

Teddy nodded. "I'll be back soon," he told Molly. "You can finish my cookies."

Teddy started out the door, but Molly stopped him. To his pleasant surprise she leaned over and gave him a gentle kiss on his cheek. Then she took a flower from her hair and stuck it in the lapel of his jacket.

Teddy looked tenderly at Molly and smiled. Then he left the apartment, as usual bumping his head on the door frame.

Coltrane was waiting outside in the garbage truck when Teddy emerged from his building. She noticed that he was singing and dancing by himself as he approached the truck.

"Singing to the stars and dancing in the street," remarked Coltrane with a knowing grin. "I'd say that was a textbook case of dino-love."

"You act like only humans fall in love," Teddy

said as he climbed behind the wheel of the truck and took a deep whiff of the flower Molly had stuck in his lapel. "Lots of animals fall in love for life. Doves, swans, and — "

"Doves and swans went extinct months ago," Coltrane reminded Teddy.

"I can't understand your species," said Teddy. "Why do you keep your feelings bottled up?"

"Finished?" asked Coltrane. Teddy could see the subject was making her uncomfortable.

"No," Teddy said firmly. "You're what we call an Anklyosaurus type. Tough exterior, soft inside. But it sure looked to me like you cared for Sebastian."

Coltrane sighed. "Why don't you just drive!" she said insistently. "We're wanted at headquarters!"

As Teddy drove away he noticed something in the rearview mirror. Six kids in hooded sweatshirts had appeared from out of nowhere and were now playing in front of his apartment building.

Funny, Teddy thought as he drove down the street, *those kids weren't there a minute ago.*

17

TEDDY'S APARTMENT, 3:30 P.M.

When Molly had finished all that was left of the macadamia chip cookies, she fixed herself one last glass of milk and swallowed it in one gulp. Then she began to feel tired. So far it had been a long, exhausting day. Not only had she said her final good-byes to Oliver, but she had fallen in love with Teddy Rex.

She decided that what she needed was a nice, warm bubble bath. So she went into Teddy's washroom and began running the water in his bathtub. She looked in the medicine cabinet, but could find no bubble bath solution. Fortunately, however, Molly always kept a little bubble bath solution in one of her earrings for just such emergencies.

In no time at all the bathtub had become filled with warm, soapy water. Molly climbed in. She could feel every dino-bone in her body relax as soon as she was engulfed in the soothing water. She became so relaxed that she started to sing.

Suddenly she heard a sound from the next room. She stopped singing. Was somebody there? Soon the washroom door slowly began to creak open. Molly felt her heart nearly stop when she saw something push through the open door.

It was only Zippy. Molly sighed with relief as Teddy's dog walked himself over to the bathtub. Then, as Molly began to sing again, Zippy sat himself down, cocked his ears, and listened.

Then, without warning, the washroom door exploded open and six small figures in hooded sweatshirts barged in. Zippy yelped. Molly cowered lower behind some bubbles. The six intruders had guns and they were all aimed at Molly.

A second later a seventh figure entered, a menacing grin on his face.

"Somebody hand Miss Rex a towel," he ordered. "She should be nice and dry when we deliver her to her new host."

And with that he let out a long, sinister laugh.

Teddy and Coltrane waited as Captain Alaric finished entering Gun assignments into his computer. He sat in a large, enveloping chair that was raised several feet off the ground by a supporting crane. Before him was a monitor nearly the size of the entire wall. It showed all the problem crime areas of the Grid and the Guns assigned to those areas. Next to the name of each Gun was the amount of credits earned from the crimes each had solved. Coltrane couldn't help noticing that her name was at the very bottom of the list.

"Ah, Coltrane," said Alaric as he lowered his chair to floor level. "You're just in time for some squeeze tea."

"Teddy Rex," said Coltrane. "Meet Captain Alaric."

"Welcome to law enforcement on the incentive plan," Alaric said to Teddy.

Teddy knew what the captain meant. The more crimes Guns solved, the more money they earned. He reached out his tail and shook Captain Alaric's hand.

"Teddy Rex, public relations, isn't it?" Alaric asked.

"Not anymore, sir."

"He was field-promoted to detective," explained Coltrane.

"Do you have anything on the murder weapon, sir?" Teddy asked the captain.

Alaric nodded and led Teddy and Coltrane to the lab table. Next to a bubbling teapot sat a small Plexiglas box that contained what appeared to be a steel butterfly.

"We ran some tests on the fragment Katie sent from the museum," said Alaric. "And I reconstructed the gizmo myself."

"A butterfly?" asked Coltrane.

"A replica," replied Alaric. "It carries an explosive charge in its body. Detonates on contact with the victim. The work of a real *artiste*."

"Gee," said Teddy as he leaned forward and took a closer look at the butterfly. He found it hard to imagine that such a small weapon could destroy a full-sized dinosaur like Oliver Rex. "Where would our killer get a weapon like this?"

"Only one name comes to mind," said Alaric. "In techno-kill circles he goes by the name of the Toymaker."

"Nasty," said Coltrane as she looked at the deadly weapon.

Alaric poured himself a bottle of tea. "This was a flash-kill, kids," he told the detectives. "A warning. So those still living take heed and don't take on airs."

"A warning to who?" asked Teddy.

Alaric took a squeeze of his tea and smiled. "I supply the 'how,'" he said. "You, the 'who.'"

"Under what rock," asked Coltrane, "do we find this Toymaker?"

19

Teddy pulled the garbage truck up in front of the big warehouse and came to a stop. Then he and Coltrane stepped out. The warehouse was the only building on a shadowy, unlit street. Across its entrance hung a badly worn sign that read: DRAGON'S TAIL STORAGE CO. — "WE ICE IT, YOU THAW IT."

Coltrane felt uneasy. The street was so desolate, she and Teddy could be taken by a surprise attacker at any given moment. She opened a secret compartment on her arm, took out a microdisk, and loaded it into a computer port in the same arm.

"Downloading," she said. "Ambush avoidance."

Teddy was stunned when he realized what Coltrane had just done. She had just given away a secret about herself that she had, up until now, kept very well hidden: She was part computer and she had a computer chip implanted in her brain. It meant that Coltrane not only had the intelligence capabilities of a computer, but that she had special radar devices as well.

"I didn't know you were a Bio-Ware," said Teddy with surprise.

"Every Gun is implanted with bio-chips," explained Coltrane. "Our motto is: *'More human than human.'*"

"That must be classified information."

"Yes. That's how Alaric wants it."

"Katie? How did you — ?" Teddy started shyly. He wanted to know how Coltrane had become a Bio-Ware, but was afraid she might be insulted if he asked.

"Years ago I intercepted a genetic code smuggler," said Coltrane. "Someone put a hit on me. Next thing I know I'm in the hospital with no chance of survival. Alaric shows up with the deal of a lifetime, literally. So, I took the Bio-Ware option and became the first of many."

"Katie, how old are you?" asked Teddy.

"I'll be seventy-five on my next birthday," replied Coltrane.

Teddy looked at his partner in amazement. She didn't look a day over thirty. "You look good," he told her. "You were lucky."

"Sometimes I don't think so," Coltrane said unhappily. "Sometimes I don't know."

"Why not?"

"Because family is not an option for Bio-Wares. There are times I wonder if I missed out."

"But Bio-Wares are perfect cops."

Coltrane paused. She had suddenly become very sad. "There may be more to life than being the perfect cop," she said. "You're ambitious. So was I. But don't let it turn you into the first dino Bio-Ware, okay?"

"Okay," agreed Teddy with a smile.

All of a sudden an enormous guard dog with fierce eyes and sharp yellow fangs leaped out from inside the building. Coltrane reached for her weapon, but Teddy stepped in front of her and growled at the dog. Upon seeing Teddy's ferocious face, the guard dog gulped, turned tail, and ran back inside the building.

Coltrane relaxed her stance, but kept her gun out in case of any more surprises. Then she and Teddy entered the dark building.

Inside was an immense room, as wide and as high as a big cavern. The room was filled with rows and rows of large rectangular boxes made out of clear Plexiglas.

Teddy's eyes had just begun to adjust to the darkness. Then, without warning, he felt so dizzy that he almost fell down. "Molly!" he cried out.

"Where?" asked Coltrane.

"My dino-sense," replied Teddy. "I felt Molly cry out for me. Something's happened to her!"

20

Teddy started for the exit.

"You can't just waltz off for your girlfriend," Coltrane said as she reached out and stopped Teddy. "We're on a case!"

"I have to!" insisted Teddy.

"Hey," said Coltrane. "I thought this was about you being a detective."

Teddy thought about this for a minute. Then he remembered something Coltrane had said herself just a few minutes earlier. She said there may be more to life than being a perfect cop. Now Teddy felt the same way. Molly was in danger and that meant more to him than anything else. He started off again.

"Oh, great," said Coltrane. "Go on! This is just what they want!"

Teddy stopped again. "'*They?*'" he asked.

"Don't you see?" asked Coltrane. "Summers put us together because he thinks we're a joke. Everybody does."

"You mean he *wants* us to mess up? But *why*?"

Coltrane shook her head. She explained to Teddy that she didn't know the answer. But she did know that the only way she and Teddy could solve this case was if they stayed in the warehouse and found the Toymaker.

Teddy understood. "I think it's time to take out the trash," he said firmly. Then he and Coltrane walked deeper into the warehouse until they reached a check-in counter. There was nobody in sight so Coltrane rang a bell on the desk that was marked: RING FOR SERVICE.

All of a sudden a metallic eyeball popped out from the desktop and looked the two detectives up and down.

"Welcome to Dragon's Tail Storage," said the eyeball, blinking once or twice as it spoke. *"Who's gonna die?"*

"Nobody," replied Teddy. "We came to talk to the Toymaker."

"Nobody here by that name!" exclaimed the eyeball. *"Go away!"*

Coltrane stepped right in front of the eyeball. "Scan my badge and think it over," she said in a threatening tone of voice.

The eyeball took a good long look at Coltrane's badge. Then, as if by magic, it sprouted two lovely butterfly wings and said: *"My apologies. Please follow me."*

A few feet away an elevator door *whooshed* open. The flying eyeball fluttered its wings a few times then led Teddy and Coltrane into the elevator. They rode the car several flights up. When the doors opened again, they found themselves before a vast room filled with all types of weapons and mounted metallic butterflies. In the center of the room a tall man in a black robe was hunched over a table absorbed in some work. It looked to Teddy and Coltrane as though he were building a small metallic beetle. As soon as they approached the table the man stood up. Teddy knew the man must be the Toymaker.

"A Bio-Ware and a dragon," said the Toymaker as soon as he saw the two visitors.

"Grid Police," said Teddy flashing his badge. "Coltrane and Teddy Rex."

"Last night one of your custom-kill toys took out a Rex," Coltrane told the Toymaker.

With that as his cue, Teddy tossed the reconstructed butterfly in front of the scientist. "With this we can connect you to the murder weapon," he said.

A look of recognition came over the Toymaker's face as soon as he saw the butterfly. "What do you wish?" he asked the detectives.

"One wish and one question," replied Coltrane.

"Wish first," said the Toymaker.

"My associate here wants a gun."

Teddy looked at Coltrane with surprise. "No, I don't!" he said.

"Yes, you do!" insisted Coltrane.

"No!"

"Look," Coltrane said, pressing her face close to Teddy's. "You're a dinosaur cop. A walking one-liner. An extinct species in an endangered profession. You need something more than ten feet of tail to help you stay alive!"

While Teddy and Coltrane squabbled, the Toymaker pressed a switch on his newly constructed metallic beetle. Unnoticed by the detectives, the beetle began to move slowly around the table in circles.

"I can't help you," the Toymaker told Coltrane.

"Look at it like this, Toymaker," Coltrane replied in a threatening tone of voice. "You're facing accessory to murder one and a long prison stay."

The Toymaker considered for a moment. Then, realizing Coltrane had the upper hand, he opened a large box filled with huge dino-sized guns and grenades.

"Here are some weapons for your partner," said the Toymaker.

"He's not my *partner*!" insisted Coltrane. Then she told Teddy to take a weapon.

But Teddy refused to take one. "I said no," he reminded her firmly.

Coltrane turned back to the Toymaker. "Tell us who chipped in for the weapon that flamed out Oliver Rex," she demanded.

The Toymaker paused. Then he suddenly leaped toward his worktable and pulled a hidden switch. All at once a trapdoor in the floor beneath him opened up and he fell through, escaping down a long chute.

Coltrane ran toward the trapdoor, but before she could reach it she heard a strange mechanical buzzing sound. The mechanical beetle the Toymaker had switched on was now zipping across the table and heading straight toward her.

"Katie, look out!" Teddy shouted out a warning, but it was too late. No sooner had Coltrane looked up than the beetle exploded with such power that the whole room began to shake!

21

The explosion had blown the lab table to bits and sent debris flying in all directions. But when the smoke cleared, Coltrane realized that she was unharmed. Teddy had covered her with his body and protected her from injury with his own thick hide.

"Are you okay?" Teddy asked.

Coltrane cleared her head. Other than a little dizziness and a slight ache in her elbow, she felt fine.

She suddenly remembered that the Toymaker had escaped down the trapdoor. "That little slug got away," she said.

Teddy smiled. Then he raised his tail from the escape chute. It was wrapped around the struggling figure of the Toymaker. Teddy had caught the Toymaker just before the explosion and now held him like a prize trout.

"Let me down!" demanded the Toymaker as he writhed and wiggled and tried to break free of Teddy's tail.

Teddy carried the Toymaker over to a great big hole in the wall that had been made by the explosion. Then he thrust the little man through the wall and dangled him over the street, several stories below.

"You remember us?" Coltrane asked the Toymaker with devilish pleasure. Now it was time for the Toymaker to be scared.

"Shall I drop him?" Teddy asked Coltrane playfully.

"Go ahead," answered Coltrane.

"No! Please don't drop me!" the Toymaker shouted fearfully. "What do you want? Name it!"

"Now *that's* what I call a positive attitude," Coltrane said. "Who did you sell your killer butterfly to?"

"His street name is Edge," answered the Toymaker.

"And where do we find him?"

"He works for Kane!"

Coltrane paused. Both she and Teddy were surprised. "Kane?" she asked. "Mr. New Eden?"

"Kane controls everything," the trembling Toymaker explained. Suddenly he felt himself slipping through Teddy's tail. "Help me!"

"Why should we?" Coltrane asked him.

"I'll tell you more!"

"Like what?"

"Word on the street is that Kane kidnapped your little friend to make you stop the dino-investigation," continued the Toymaker. "It's some boy who works at a mystery meat stand!"

Coltrane felt her heart leap as she realized the Toymaker was talking about Sebastian. "Where is Kane?" she demanded.

"In his compound. It's like a fortress."

"New Eden?" asked Teddy.

"How do we get in?" asked Coltrane.

"Talk to his henchmen," answered the Toymaker, without taking his frightened eyes off the street below. "The Zapheads. Only they can help you."

"Why's that?"

"Because Kane cloned the Zapheads. He only trusts those he creates! They can get you in."

Coltrane realized that she had learned everything she needed to know and signaled to Teddy with a wink. Teddy pulled the Toymaker back into the room. Then they tied him up, attached a special tracking device to his clothes, and radioed headquarters to order a backup unit to collect the Toymaker.

Teddy and Coltrane lost no time as they raced outside and drove off in their truck. Teddy knew that Molly was in trouble. Earlier his dino-sense had told him so. Images had flashed through his mind, clear visions of Molly being kidnapped by a menacing group wearing hooded sweatshirts. They were the same group he had seen playing outside his apartment as he drove away earlier that night. They were also the same group that had attacked him in front of the Extinct Species Club the night before, the same group that had trashed the Rex Cruiser. Now he knew who they were: *Zapheads*. He realized that Kane must have ordered them to kidnap Molly. But why?

Coltrane was familiar with the Zapheads' hangout, the basement of an abandoned tenement building in one of the oldest sections of the Grid. She shouted directions to Teddy as they raced through the streets in their garbage truck.

In no time at all they reached the abandoned building and cautiously got out of the truck.

Coltrane drew her gun and carefully tiptoed down a stairway that led to the entrance of the basement. Teddy followed closely behind. Through a dusty window they could see the Zapheads. They were sitting around eating pizzas and listening to loud *rusty metal* music. There were seven of them, including their leader, who Coltrane recognized as Spinner.

Coltrane kicked the door inward and entered, her gun aimed at the shocked Zapheads.

"Don't anybody stand up," she ordered. "We're here to trade your necks for weapons, a ride, and a meeting with your boss."

Just then Spinner snapped his fingers and the

Zapheads pulled out a variety of powerful-looking laser pistols, machine guns, and flame throwers. Coltrane was outnumbered.

"Who's *'we'*?" asked Spinner with a sinister snarl.

"Me," answered Coltrane, without flinching.

" — and *me!*" came a voice from the shadows. The Zapheads turned around. Teddy had snuck up behind them. *WHAP!* He swept his tail under their feet and felled them as if they were bowling pins.

Coltrane stepped forward.

"Now," she said firmly. "*We* want Kane."

Deputy Commissioner Summers sat in Mr. Kane's office and looked out the window at the New Eden compound below. He had been summoned to the office by Dr. Shade. He knew that could mean only one thing: Mr. Kane's secret plan was about to begin.

He knew he had done his part well by assigning Teddy Rex and Katie Coltrane together. They were the two most bumbling members of the Grid Police Department. He was certain they would never discover that Mr. Kane was the one responsible for the murder of Oliver Rex.

Summers had done a great service for Mr. Kane. He knew that now was the time for Mr. Kane to pay him back.

While in the middle of these thoughts, Summers heard a door in the office open and saw Dr. Shade enter. Dr. Shade smiled politely at Summers and invited him to sit down in a chair in front of Mr. Kane's desk.

"You've been helpful, Mr. Summers," said Dr. Shade. "New Eden needs more like you."

"Well?" Summers asked anxiously. "When do I get a seat on the ark?"

"Excuse me?" asked Dr. Shade.

"Mr. Kane promised me immortality," replied Summers. "I mean that's what this flea circus is all about, right?"

Dr. Shade reached over and took a reading of Summers's pulse.

"Tell me," she began. "What diseases run in your family?"

"Just flat feet and buck teeth," replied Summers. He secretly laughed to himself, happy with the knowledge that he had no illnesses that would interfere with Mr. Kane's plan for a new and pure world.

Dr. Shade smiled at Summers. Then she pressed a hidden button underneath Mr. Kane's desktop. Without warning, a ray flashed across Summers's body and flash-froze him just like the ice fish in Mr. Kane's fish tank.

As soon as that was done the side door opened again. This time Mr. Kane himself came into the office. He smiled at Dr. Shade.

"Dispose of him," he ordered.

Dr. Shade nodded and pressed another button on the desk. Suddenly the frozen figure of Deputy Summers splintered into a million tiny fragments of ice and fell on the floor. In a few short seconds the shards of ice began to melt until there was nothing left of Summers but a shallow puddle of water.

Next Mr. Kane stepped over to the wall and pressed a button. A second later a console with a large viewing screen rolled forward. Kane turned on the viewing screen and a map of the earth appeared. Then he began to press a series of switches on the console. For each switch he pressed, a light appeared over a different country on the map.

"Switching down?" Dr. Shade asked her boss.

"Just switching to manual," replied Mr. Kane. Then he pulled a small remote-control device from his pocket and pointed it at the console. An evil smile came over his face.

Dr. Shade smiled, too. So far their plan had gone without a hitch.

At that instant the sound of alarms and sirens filled the room. Kane and Dr. Shade knew at once that an intruder had gotten into the complex. Dr. Shade reached for the holophone and dialed security, but before she could get an answer the entire room began to rumble as if in an earthquake.

CRASH! Teddy and Coltrane burst through the

wall in their garbage truck. Glass and truck parts flew haphazardly with the debris. Before the dust had a chance to settle, Teddy and Coltrane pulled themselves from the wreckage. Then Teddy unrolled his tail to reveal they had a prisoner with them. It was Spinner, the boss Zaphead.

"You little squid," Dr. Shade said to Spinner as he rolled out on the floor before her and Mr. Kane.

"Please," Spinner pleaded with Mr. Kane. He was trembling with fright. "They made me bring them in!"

Dr. Shade pulled out a gun and zapped Spinner, vaporizing him instantly. Then she turned the gun toward Teddy, but Coltrane was too fast. She leaped into the air and knocked Dr. Shade out cold with a ninja kick. Now she trained her own gun on Mr. Kane.

"Where's Molly?" Teddy demanded of Kane.

"Where's Sebastian?" demanded Coltrane.

"In a cage where he belongs," replied Kane.

Coltrane stepped threateningly toward Kane. "Where is this cage?" she asked with determination.

"In my zoo."

"Watch the Mad Hatter," Coltrane told Teddy. "I'll get Sebastian." Then Coltrane climbed over the wreckage and debris and made her way out of the room. When she was gone, Teddy and Kane faced each other.

"You let me down, Teddy," said Kane.

"Sorry to disappoint you," said Teddy, sarcastically. After all, it was Kane who had let *him* down.

"Sometimes parents are disappointed in their children," said Kane.

"Oliver was your child," Teddy retorted. "You created him just like you did me."

"Yes," admitted Kane. "Unfortunately, his sacrifice was necessary."

"At headquarters we call it murder," said Teddy.

"Words," laughed Kane. "To create destiny takes faith. Life is in actions."

"Yes," agreed Teddy. "And you're going to pay for yours."

"Oh, really? Why? Because I broke one of your silly laws put there to protect the weak? Don't be silly."

"You're under arrest," said Teddy, without thinking he was being silly at all.

Kane pressed a button on his remote control. Teddy watched as the wall behind the map console spread open to reveal another, larger room. In the room were rows and rows of sleek, shiny rockets. They looked to Teddy to be missiles. And they were all aimed skyward.

"In a few minutes," Kane told Teddy, "my neutronium missiles will put humanity out of its misery forever!"

Then he let out a long, maniacal laugh as he aimed his remote control at the missiles and brought his finger down on the launch button.

Mr. Kane had moved so fast that there was nothing Teddy could do to stop him.

23

Teddy watched with horror as, one by one, the missiles were launched and soared through an opening in the ceiling.

"And the billions of innocent people?" Teddy asked Mr. Kane anxiously, his eyes fixed with alarm.

"A failed species," replied Kane. "There is no room for imperfection in my New World."

Teddy suddenly realized what Kane meant. His missiles would destroy everything that existed outside New Eden.

"Softskins may be rough around the edges," said Teddy, "but it's part of their charm."

"No!" insisted Kane. "It's their fatal flaw! This time I will run evolution my way!"

"You're seriously stressed," observed Teddy.

"History always misunderstands visionaries like myself," said Kane.

"I think they call you monsters," commented Teddy.

Kane reached over and pulled a lever. Another wall gave way, revealing a vast ship behind it.

"This is my Ark," he told Teddy. "It contains the seeds of the New Eden."

Teddy gasped in amazement. The Ark was immense, at least the size of a small Grid block. Zapheads were busy loading the great ship with all the different species of animals that Teddy had seen roaming around the compound grounds on his previous visit to New Eden.

"I have brought here pairs of all the planet's insects, mammals, amphibians, birds, bacteria, etcetera, etcetera," Kane continued. "The ingredients for paradise."

"So each time a species went extinct, it was because you swiped the animals?" Teddy said, realizing at once why there had been such a sudden rash of extinctions in recent months.

"A small price to give them immortality, don't you think?"

"But why?"

"For you."

Teddy was confused. "Me?"

"Yes," answered Kane. "And Molly is your reward."

Molly! Teddy was filled with dread. "What have you done with her?" he demanded, raising his tail to show that he meant to get an answer.

Kane was not frightened. "You'll see her soon enough," he said. "I'm pleased that you care for each other. This has worked out better than I hoped."

"It has?"

"You see," Kane began to explain, "I needed pairs of all animals. Rexes included. Oliver worked in Species Records and he became aware of my plan. He called me insane."

"That's a surprise?" remarked Teddy.

"That naive dino had the nerve to threaten me and expose my plan to the world," continued Kane. "Since he had access to the records, measures had to be taken."

"So you had him killed," said Teddy, now realizing the full truth.

"Nature's oldest law, my son," Kane confessed. "Survival of the fittest."

Suddenly Teddy felt a cold piece of metal against his head. It was Edge. And he had a gun.

"Take care of him," Kane ordered Edge. Then he ran to the missile console and monitored the missiles as they headed toward Earth's orbit.

"Good-bye, cruel world," said Teddy, closing his eyes and thinking this was the end.

But Edge didn't pull the trigger. Instead, Teddy heard a wall on the Ark slide open. He opened his eyes and saw a laboratory that housed two dinosaur-sized Plexiglas chambers with tubes running in and out of them. One of the chambers was empty. In the other was Molly.

"Molly!" Teddy shouted happily. But Molly couldn't hear him. She seemed frozen, as if in a state of suspended animation. Then Teddy remembered the ice fish that Kane had shown him and realized that Molly had been flash-frozen.

Edge pressed a remote-control button and the door on the empty chamber next to Molly's opened up. Then he nudged Teddy forward with his gun.

Teddy got the idea. Edge wanted him to step into the empty chamber. He was going to be flash-frozen, too!

24

Coltrane looked out from behind the bushes and watched the cage where Sebastian was being held prisoner. She had scoured the compound looking for him, doing her best to avoid Zapheads along the way. Now that she'd found him, she smiled. He didn't look harmed or undernourished and he had even made friends with a tiny monkey that was sharing his cage.

Coltrane noticed that three Zapheads were standing guard in front of the cage. Each one had a flash gun. Thinking quickly, Coltrane snuck up and hid in a shadow next to the cage.

"Mr. Kane wants the boy brought to his office," she said in her best imitation Zaphead voice.

The Zapheads turned to see who was talking. Coltrane took one step forward, out of the shadow. The Zapheads lifted their flash guns, but

Coltrane was too fast. She drew her weapon first and zapped them one by one before they had a chance to fire.

"Katie!" Sebastian exclaimed happily.

"Hiya, kid," said Coltrane as she stepped over the Zapheads and shot open the cage door lock with her gun. "How you doing?"

"I've been worse." Sebastian smiled as he hugged Coltrane hello. Then he motioned to his new friend, the little monkey. The monkey jumped onto his shoulder, and both of them followed Coltrane away from the cage.

25

"You murdered Oliver, didn't you?" Teddy accused Edge as he inched his way toward the empty cryogenic chamber in the Ark lab.

"The dino?" asked Edge. "Yes."

"Why?" asked Teddy.

"Why *not*?" replied Edge sinisterly.

"Because . . ." Teddy stopped and acted as if he was going to give an answer, but instead, swept his tail up and sent Edge flying into the ceiling. Edge's gun sailed across the room. Then Edge fell to the ground, unconscious.

Now Teddy saw his chance to set Molly free. He pressed several buttons on her chamber, but nothing happened. She remained frozen.

"No!" Teddy cried.

Teddy didn't know what to do. He had to get Molly out of that chamber. He began to pound on the glass chamber. Not a moment later Molly began to stir, awakened by the rattling. Then she opened her eyes.

"Theo?" she asked, tenderly raising her claw.

"Molly!" Teddy exclaimed happily. He placed his hand on the chamber's glass exactly where Molly's claw was. Then he opened the chamber and helped her out. Happy to see each other again, they hugged.

"What is this place?" a familiar voice came from behind them.

Teddy turned around and smiled. It was Coltrane. And Sebastian was with her, too.

"It looks like some weird zoo!" Sebastian said as he looked at the Ark in wonder.

"It's Mr. Kane's Ark," said another voice. Teddy and the others looked toward the entrance to the Ark. This time it was Dr. Shade who spoke.

"How do we stop the missiles?" Teddy demanded.

Dr. Shade smiled. "Only Mr. Kane can do that," she answered.

Coltrane reached out and grabbed Dr. Shade by the arm. "Really?" Then she pushed Dr. Shade into one of the empty cryogenic chambers.

"Yes," replied Dr. Shade. "He carries his remote control at all times."

"Nightie-night," Coltrane said as she pressed a button on Dr. Shade's chamber. *WHOOSH!* Dr. Shade became flash-frozen inside.

"*GOOD-BYE, THEODORE!*" screamed a voice from above.

Teddy looked up. It was Mr. Kane. He was staring down at them from a catwalk that overlooked the Ark. In his hand was a flash gun aimed right at Teddy!

BOOM! BOOM! BOOM! Mr. Kane fired three shots, but missed. Teddy grabbed Molly and dived behind a table. Coltrane jumped in front of Sebastian, pulling her gun out as she did so. She fired back at Kane, hitting him in the arm.

Kane winced. Then he aimed his gun at Coltrane and returned her fire, hitting her once in the shoulder. Coltrane fell back instantly, grabbing her shoulder as she fell to the ground. When Teddy and the others reached her, they saw that she was bleeding badly.

"You're one great detective, *partner*," Coltrane told Teddy weakly.

"*Partner?*" asked Teddy. It was the first time Coltrane ever called him that.

"Sorry I was such a — " Coltrane started, but a shot of pain kept her from finishing.

"Katie?" Teddy asked. He was worried. Coltrane did not look so good.

A second later she closed her eyes and slumped over.

"No!" cried Sebastian as he looked down at Coltrane's face.

Teddy felt angry. Mr. Kane had gone too far. Coltrane was more than just his partner, she was his friend.

He grabbed Coltrane's gun.

Gun in hand, he raced up the stairs that led to the catwalk that overlooked the Ark. But by the time he had gotten to the top, Kane had fled.

Teddy looked down the catwalk. A door at the far end swung shut just as he arrived. Teddy ran along the catwalk and through the door. Another stairway led downward to another door. Now the second door was swinging shut.

Teddy took a deep breath and leaped off the top step. He landed, on both feet, with a thud on the floor below. Then he went through the second door.

Teddy paused. He had emerged back outside on the New Eden compound, but Kane was nowhere to be seen. Then he noticed something on the ground. A trail of blood droplets led down the street.

No sooner had Teddy started to follow the crimson trail than a shot rang out. Teddy fell backwards as he felt a flash bullet hit him in the chest. Seconds later he looked up to see Kane standing over him with a gun.

"You . . ." Teddy began groggily. "You're under arrest . . ."

Kane laughed. "You must learn to accept defeat," Kane said with a malicious smile.

Teddy then lifted the gun he had taken from Coltrane and aimed it at Kane.

For some reason, Kane was not frightened. "You can't do it," he told Teddy. "Violence is against your genetic code. I know. I created you."

"Drop . . . the . . . gun . . ." Teddy said, struggling against his own nature.

"You can't be what you're not, Theodore," said Kane.

Teddy squeezed the trigger anyway, only the gun didn't fire. It was empty.

Kane laughed maniacally. Then he climbed into a New Eden Jeep, turned on the headlights and stepped on the gas. Teddy was on the ground directly in the Jeep's path. Kane accelerated and began driving full speed toward the helpless Rex.

Teddy looked up. His head was still dizzy from the flash gunshot. He could barely make out the two headlights that were racing toward him.

A tree was just a few inches away from where Teddy lay. Thinking quickly, Teddy whipped his tail around the tree and pulled himself out of the path of the oncoming Jeep just seconds before being crushed. Rising to his feet he changed the setting on his pistol for PITON and raised it toward the Jeep as it receded down the street.

BANG! He fired. This time the gun worked! A sharp metal grappling hook and rope shot out and caught on Kane's coat. Teddy pulled on the rope and yanked Kane out of the Jeep. Then Teddy reeled him in as if he were a big fish.

Seconds later Kane's remote control fell to the ground. Now was Teddy's chance. He grabbed the remote and pressed the button marked MISSILE ABORT.

From where he was he couldn't hear them, but Teddy knew that Kane's neutronium missiles had just exploded harmlessly in outer space.

Teddy had saved the world.

27

A few days later, after Mr. Kane had been put in jail, the New Eden Compound had been changed into a public zoo. A sign at the entrance read: NEW EDEN ZOO — OPEN TO THE PUBLIC. Kids from all over the Grid had come to see the animals they had once thought to be extinct.

As a special opening day event, the entire Grid Police Department gathered for a special ceremony in the zoo. Commissioner Lynch stood on a podium. Standing with him was Teddy, his wounds bandaged, dressed in a suit and tie. Next to Teddy, alive and well, stood Coltrane.

"Theodore Rex," Commissioner Lynch said to Teddy, his voice sounding over loudspeakers in all parts of the zoo. "It's my honor to promote you to Detective, First Class."

Commissioner Lynch presented Teddy with an oversized badge. They shook hand and tail.

"You were right, Teddy," he whispered. "We *can* rise above and make our dreams come true."

Teddy looked down at the audience where Molly Rex was watching all this and smiled proudly.

Next, the commissioner turned to Coltrane. "And Katie Coltrane," he said, "I accept your resignation from the Gun Command. And for rising to the occasion, I transfer you to the public relations department." Then he leaned over and whispered to her: "Just go easy on the public."

"I'll try, sir," replied Coltrane happily. Then she glanced down at the audience and smiled warmly at Sebastian, who was seated next to Molly Rex.

"Theodore Rex and Katie Coltrane," continued Commissioner Lynch. "We owe you an apology. *Scale. Softskin.* You've shown us they're only words. Words that keep us apart. Our destiny rests on all species treating each other with compassion, kindness, and respect."

At that the entire Grid Police Force cheered.

As the ceremony came to a close, Teddy turned to Coltrane. "You got my old job," he said.

"Yeah," replied Coltrane happily. "I'm working my way *down* the ladder of success!"

And with that Coltrane extended her hand to Teddy's tail and they shook on it.